This book unfortunately belongs to:

_____

This book is dedicated to baskets...

...for holding everyone's eggs.

ackersbooks.com

Entire World Books: 11

Copyright Joey and Melanie Acker 2022
Ackers' Books, LLC

Melanie was too busy hangin' with her peeps to help.

ISBN–13: 978–1–951046–36–1

The WORST EASTER Book

in the Whole Entire World

Joey Acker

Greetings.

or perhaps not...

BECAUSE THIS IS
THE WORST EASTER BOOK IN THE
WHOLE ENTIRE WORLD!

Wouldn't you rather go on a super fun Easter Egg Hunt than read this horribly ridiculous book?!?

Really? You're still reading this book?

Very well. I guess I'll tell you why this is the
worst Easter book in the whole entire world...

Reason #1: I actually like Easter, but I'm stuck in this book talking to you instead of looking for eggs filled with wonderful treasures and CANDY inside!

Reason #2: I don't understand where the Easter Bunny gets all those eggs. Bunnies don't lay eggs...

What animal lays eggs?

BOCK
BOCK

What was that?

I'm Gary the Easter Chicken!

Reason #3: There is no Easter Chicken!

Reason #4: There is an Easter Chicken!
I AM the Easter Chicken! AND I am tired of
the "Easter" bunny stealing all of my eggs!!!

I am so confused right now…

Think about it, rock.

Where do you think a RABBIT gets all of
those EGGS?

Reason #5: He's actually got a point.

Listen, I just want the world to know the truth. Every year it's "Easter Bunny this, Easter Bunny that!" No one ever talks or even knows about the Easter Chicken!

I probably would have picked a better book to tell everyone in...

Hold on...so you have Easter eggs
with wonderful treasures and
candy inside?!?

I did, but that dirty rotten rabbit
steals them all every single year!

Hey!

Do you want to help me get my eggs back and tell the whole entire world the truth about the "Easter" bunny?!?

Do I really have a choice?

Nope!

Reason #6: The author is making me go along! This is NOT my idea of an Easter egg hunt!

I am sooooooo glad you are helping me!

This is going to be MY year!

AHHHHHHH!

Your year is looking
pretty dark, Gary...

The ground must have collapsed
and we fell!

At least we're here!

Where is 'here'?!?

The rotten rabbit's lair!

Maybe this isn't such a good idea...

Just relax!

I don't think anyone is
even here.

You thought wrong,
Gary…

Why are you in my house,
chicken?

My name is
GARY THE **EASTER** CHICKEN,
and I am here because YOU steal
MY eggs every year!!!

Easter Chicken?!?

This world is only big enough
for one Easter creature and
that creature is ME!

Reason #7: I'm pretty sure this conversation and entire book is completely missing the meaning of Easter...

but then again...it is the worst...

Why do you steal
all of my eggs?

Because I got tired of always
getting pecked on!

You have got to be kidding me.

Do you mean **'picked'** on?

I was picked on by being pecked, pulled, and pushed every time I passed Pepper's Produce Property to pluck precious prickly pears!

Easter Bunny,
I am so sorry! I should never have
chosen to be like those cheap childish
chickens who cheated you out of
those precious prickly pears!

What just happened?

Gary the Easter Chicken,
I forgive you and your chicken crew.

I also have a pretty sweet idea…

This must be reason #8...

EASTER CREATURE TEAM UP!

HAPPY EASTER!

The End

Made in the USA
Monee, IL
28 March 2023

30649857R00029